Lights! Camera! Hammerhead!

READ ALL THE SHARK SCHOOL BOOKS!

#1: Deep-Sea Disaster

COMING SOON

#3: Squid-napped!

SHARK SCHOOL

#2 Lights! Camera! Hammerhead!

BY DAVY OCEAN
ILLUSTRATED BY AARON BLECHA

ALADDIN New York London Toronto Sydney New Delhi

WiTH THANKS TO PAUL EBBS

ALADDIN
An imprint of Simon & Schuster Children's Publishing Division
1230 Avenue of the Americas, New York, NY 10020
First Aladdin paperback edition May 2014
Text and concept copyright © 2013 by Hothouse Fiction
Illustrations copyright © 2013 by Aaron Blecha
All rights reserved, including the right of reproduction in whole or in part in any form.
ALADDIN is a trademark of Simon & Schuster, Inc., and related logo is a
registered trademark of Simon & Schuster, Inc.
Also available in an Aladdin hardcover edition.
For information about special discounts for bulk purchases, please contact
Simon & Schuster Special Sales at 1-866-506-1949 or business@simonandschuster.com.
The Simon & Schuster Speakers Bureau can bring authors to your live event. For more information or
to book an event contact the Simon & Schuster Speakers Bureau at 1-866-248-3049
or visit our website at www.simonspeakers.com.
The text of this book was set in Write Demibd.
Manufactured in the United States of America 1214 OFF
4 6 8 10 9 7 5 3
Library of Congress Control Number 2014933088
ISBN 978-1-4814-0682-6 (hc)
ISBN 978-1-4814-0681-9 (pbk)
ISBN 978-1-4814-0683-3 (eBook)

CHAPTER 1

"Open wider!" Ralph yells.

"Ahh caaaaaannn't!" I splutter.

"Open wider!"

"Ahh said, ahh caaaaaannn't!"

"What?"

"Ghet zout ov muh mouf!"

Ralph swims out of my mouth and

1

frowns at me. "Harry, I can't understand what you're saying. Why are you speaking in code?"

Now that Ralph is out of my mouth, I can speak normally again. "I can't open my mouth wider!" I say. "If you went in any farther, you'd be able to shake fins with my rear!"

It's the first day of the school vacation and my best friends, Joe and Ralph, and I are supposed to be on our way to Shark Park. But Joe has made us stop so he can go into Kois "R" Us for the latest set of koi carp cards, and Ralph has taken the opportunity for a feed.

Ralph narrows his eyes. "How else am I supposed to get my breakfast? I'm a pilot fish, and pilot fish eat the leftover food from between sharks' teeth. It's how we've always done it, and I don't see why we should change now."

"I'm not saying we should change it. I just don't want to swallow you!"

3

Ralph flicks his tail angrily. "Well, if you'd saved me some of your prawn flakes in your front teeth, maybe I wouldn't have to go searching the back of your mouth for bits of last night's dinner."

I poke around at the back of my mouth with my tongue and flip out two pieces of yesterday's clamburger. Ralph gobbles them up greedily, then floats in front of me, looking hopeful.

"That's all there is," I say as Joe swims out of the store empty tentacled. "They don't get the new cards in till tomorrow," Joe says miserably.

"Well, I'm going to need something

else to stop my tummy from rumbling," Ralph moans. "Half a prawn flake and two crumbs of clamburger aren't enough for a growing pilot fish."

Ralph and Joe swim off toward Shark Park. I hope they cheer up before we get there. Vacations are supposed to be fun, but they're not if your best friends are moping around like a couple of bluefish.

As we get to the park gates Joe turns to me. "Do we have to go in?" he asks gloomily. "I still haven't recovered from what happened last time."

Ralph starts to giggle at the memory

and, I have to admit, it was pretty funny. What happened last time was this:

1. Joe jumped on the wrecked-ship's-wheel merry-go-round, but he hadn't realized how fast it was going.

2. He came flying off.

3. He shot right up the slime-algae slide THE WRONG WAY . . .

4. He catapulted around the whale-rib swings SIXTEEN times, and then . . .

5. He landed with a huge TWANG on the seahorse-on-a-spring . . .

6. Which BOINGED him right up toward the surface of the sea like an out-of-control jellycopter!

If it hadn't been for Ralph and me swimming up as fast as we could to catch him, Joe would have plopped right out into the air. And everyone knows how bad being in the air is for a jelly-fish—the heat of the sun can turn them crispy in seconds.

Joe eyes the sign by the gate suspi-ciously. The sign says SHARK PARK— FAMILY FUN FOR EVERYONE!

"Hmm, I don't call being spun around like my mom's laundry fun," Joe mutters. "I don't call being thrown through the water upside down fun!"

I decide not to tell Joe that watching

him get flung around the park was fun for Ralph and me.

I look around Shark Park—at the merry-go-round, the slide, the swings, and the seahorse—and then I look at Joe, who is

folding each of his arms over the other.
One by one. This is going to take a
very long time, so I hold up a fin. "Okay,
okay," I say, "we'll do something else."

To be honest, I don't know why I suggested Shark Park in the first place. It's vacation for all the kids in Shark Point, not just us three. That means the place is stuffed to the gills with fish and sharks and dolphins and octopi. So I turn back to Ralph and Joe. "It's already full," I say. "It'll be ages before we can get on the whale-rib swings, and they're the best thing in the park." Ralph and Joe nod, so I continue. "We're all too old to go on the seahorse-on-a-spring." Ralph nods. Joe hides behind Ralph, and his bottom toots. I know he's trying to be brave, but the Seahorse TWANGING incident did

scare him quite a bit. "The only thing left for us to do would be to go and play on the sea grass, but lots of girl fish—"

"Yuck," say Joe and Ralph together at the mention of girls.

"—are playing flounders." (Flounders is like baseball but you hit a sea urchin with a bat made from a swordfish nose.)

I don't tell Ralph and Joe my last reason for wanting to leave, because I don't want to look like a scaredy-catfish. Rick Reef and Donny Dogfish are bound to be in Shark Park today, and I really don't want to swim into them. Rick is a black-tip reef shark in our class at school, and

his favorite subject is trying to annoy me. He is very good at it. In fact, you could say he is an A student when it comes to making fun of hammerheads.

Ralph and Joe nod in agreement.

"Staying in Shark Park is going to be boring," says Ralph.

"And probably deadly," Joe adds grimly. So we turn around and head back into Shark Point.

The town is swarming with kids too— all just as bored as we are.

We fin our way down the main street. There are complaining fish being dragged into stores by their moms, and a bunch

of tough-looking scallops hanging out on the corner of Coral Drive. They're try-ing to be cool by blowing toots out of the sides of their shells in tune to the music coming out of Anchovy's Arcade. The three of us swim past them pretty quickly, hoping not to catch their eye.

As I watch a kid dolphin being yelled at by his grumpy-looking dad I realize that it could be a lot worse. At least I get to hang out with my friends. At least I'm not being dragged around town by my dad. Luckily, my dad is mayor of Shark Point so he hardly ever gets any time off. Which means I never have to be dragged around by him during school break. I can't imagine anything worse.

Except . . .

"Harrrrrrrrrrrrrrrrrrrrrrrrrrrrry!"

Suddenly I can.

Oh no!

It's Mom! She's swimming as fast as

she can toward us. "I thought you boys were going to Shark Park," she says as she reaches us, taking a large polka-dotted handkerchief from her finbag and wiping something off my lip.

"Booger," she whispers. But she might as well have shouted it. Ralph and Joe both heard, and they're laughing so hard behind their fins and tentacles that I think they might choke.

Mom then makes it even worse by grabbing my fin and pulling me away. "Well, since you're not in the park, you can come with me to see your dad opening the center."

My tummy sinks twenty fathoms and I try to pull away, but Mom is holding me too tight. All I can see ahead is Mom pulling me along, and all I can hear behind is Ralph and Joe giggling.

Mom and Dad always want me to come and see him opening stuff and making speeches. Usually, I can find a way out of it, but not this time. Now I wish we'd stayed in Shark Park!

We turn a corner onto Starfish Square, and I see a huge crowd of fish and squid cheering outside the gleaming new Shark Point Sports Center. There is a flag billowing from the roof and banners hung above the door. *Click! Click! Click!* Electric-eel photographers flash their electric-eel tail cameras at the doors of the sports center as my dad proudly swims to the front of the crowd.

He waves his fin and taps his nose on the waiting microphone to make sure it's working.

Mom finally lets go of me so she can clap her fins and whistle at Dad. Seriously, I don't know where to look. I can feel my cheeks start to turn red as Ralph and Joe look at me and back to Dad. Dad is a popular mayor, but he can be really embarrassing sometimes. Ralph and Joe know this, and I can see they're waiting for him to say or do something stupid so they can pull my fin about it for the rest of the week.

Mom just keeps waving at Dad and

pointing at me so that he can see I'm here.

Dad waves back enthusiastically, and the eels all turn their cameras on me! I can feel myself turning redder than the reddest red snapper as Mom throws her fin around me and tells me to "smiley-wile." That's when Ralph and Joe fall over backward and almost die from laughing. This is the worst thing EVER!

"Yes, um, well—hello!" shouts Dad in his usual absentminded way. "Um, yes, well, I would like to welcome you all here today . . ."

Don't do it!

"But before we begin . . ."

Dad. Please. Don't do it!

"I'd just like to say that seeing you all here has reminded me . . ."

Nope. He's going to do it. He's going to tell one of his awful jokes. I try to hide under Ralph and Joe.

"Why did the deaf frog come to hear my speech today?"

Silence.

"Because"—and here Dad chuckles to himself—"because he thought I was going to be opening a Warts Center!"

No one laughs besides Mom. But Dad doesn't realize that his joke has gone down quicker than the *Titanic* and just continues as if nothing has happened. "So I duly declare the Shark Point Sports Center o—"

A piece of yellow seaweed drifts toward Dad's face and catches him in the eye. As he raises a fin to wipe it away, he accidentally slices the OPENING TODAY! ribbon that's stretched across the doors. Before he has a chance to say "—pen!" he is bounced out of the way by the rushing crowd and sent spinning up to the roof of the center, where he gets tangled in the flag and stuck to the flagpole!

I watch in horror as the photographers focus their cameras on Dad. Mom squeals and swims up to try and untangle him from the flagpole as the cameras flash and flash and flash.

I know what's going to be on the front page of the *Seaweed Times* tomorrow—my dad wrapped around the flagpole like a shark kebab. And that means every-one in Shark Point is going to be laugh-ing at him. And laughing at me

for having such an embarrassing dad!

I pull Joe and Ralph away.

I have to pull them because they've been laughing so much they've forgotten how to swim.

It's not until we're all the way on the other side of town by the movie theater that their laughing stops. And finally I see something that cheers me up.

Outside the movie theater is a huge poster of Gregor the Gnasher's first movie, *Parrot Fish of the Caribbean*, in which he plays Captain Jack Sprat, the action hero. In the poster he's wrestling with a giant squid. Gregor is my

total hero. Mom calls him 'that tooth-head', but she doesn't understand— he's the Underwater Wrestling Champion of the World and now he's started making movies. He's a total legend. It must be so cool to be a famous great white. I bet Gregor's kids don't ever get embarrassed by him.

I would have said, *Let's go and see the movie!* but I haven't gotten my allowance yet, and with Dad currently stuck on the roof of the sports center, it wasn't about to happen anytime soon. So we keep swimming until eventually, with nowhere else to go and nothing else to do, we end up outside the library.

"The library?" says Ralph. "Talk about double boring."

"Well, what else can we do?" I say.

Thankfully, Joe comes to my rescue. "It's probably the safest place to go," he says. "Unless, of course, a bookcase falls on our heads."

I slap a fin across my face. It would

be less work to be in school! But I lead them both inside anyway.

At least there's no chance of running into Rick and Donny in the library. Rick's only interest in books is how hard he can throw them at my hammerhead when Mrs. Shelby isn't looking.

So now we're sitting in the silent library, too bored to even pick up a book.

"Is it lunchtime yet?" Ralph whispers, looking at my teeth.

"The edges of those books look quite sharp," Joe mumbles, twiddling his tentacles nervously. "I think we'd better just sit here and not move."

Great. It's the first day of vacation and we're stuck in the library doing impressions of rocks.

I sigh, and try to think of something cool to do in silence that doesn't involve moving.

When . . .

"Wooooooooooooooooooooooooooooooooooooooooooooooooo!!!"

The shriek shatters the quiet, and I spin around in my chair, expecting to see Rick Reef waving a spider crab in front of a kid squid or something. But it's not, it's Pearl and Cora, the dolphin twins. They're dancing around

and around, high-finning and shriek-
ing, looking at their aqua-phones, looking at each other, then looking back
at their aqua-phones, then looking at
each other and . . .

"Wooooooooooooooooooooooooooooo-
ooooooooooooooooooooooo!!!"-ing again.

The librarian, Mr.
Gape, an elderly
basking shark,
heaves himself
out of his chair
and swims over
to Pearl and
Cora. "Will you

two please be quiet? This is a library, not an amusement park!"

"But—" says Pearl.

"There's—" says Cora.

Mr. Gape holds up a huge fin to shush them. "Not another word, or I must ask you to leave."

"We were leaving anyway," says Pearl.

"Oh really?" says Mr. Gape.

"Yes," says Cora. "We've got somewhere way more interesting to go than this boring old library!"

"And what, may I ask, could be more interesting than a library?" Mr. Gape

bellows, causing several people to drop their books in shock.

"Something," Pearl says, her voice rising toward another shriek, "that we've just seen on the interwet!"

"What?" demands Mr. Gape.

"Leggy air-breathers! They've been spotted just off Shark Point, and they're making a *movie*! Woooooooooooooooooooooooooo!!!" Pearl and Cora rush past us, spinning Joe around three times and knocking Ralph and me down in their wake.

But I don't care about getting knocked over. I have too many things on my mind.

1. A movie?

2. A movie????

3. (And every OTHER number!) A MOVIE????

This vacation just got interesting!!!!

CHAPTER 2

"Let's go," I say the minute Pearl and Cora leave the building.

Joe looks at me and frowns. "I want to stay here with the nice, safe books!"

I look at Ralph.

"Who wants to see a movie being made?" he says lamely. "I don't, movies are like books that move, and we know how boring books are. I think I'd rather stay here with all the . . . books . . . " His voice trails off, not being able to think of any more mindless reasons not to leave the library. Ralph's been afraid of leggy air-breathers ever since he accidentally got caught in one of their nets.

"We'll just go and take a look, okay?" I say. "We won't go anywhere near the leggies, I promise. Cross my swim bladder and hope to fry."

Ralph isn't convinced, but I'm desperate to follow Cora and Pearl. "I will keep you both totally and utterly and completely safe."

"Do you promise?" says Joe.

I nod my hammerhead—and nearly knock Mr. Gape over. "I promise. And afterward I'll go and get something to eat," I add, looking at Ralph.

Ralph's eyes glaze over hungrily. "Will you get sardine nuggets?"

I nod.

"With a portion of plankton?"

"Yes. With a portion of plankton."

"A super-size portion of plankton?"

"Yes!" I say impatiently. If we don't get going, we'll never catch up with Pearl and Cora.

"All right, then," says Ralph reluctantly.

"All right, then," says Joe, even more reluctantly.

But I don't care how reluctant they are—they've said yes and that's all that counts.

And now we're going to see a movie being made. A *movie*! How cool is that? My heart leaps like a bar of soap from wet fins at the thought!

I speed down the street, refusing to let go of Joe. Ralph is doing his best to keep up, but because he's such a little fish he can't kick as hard as I can, so I wrap my free fin around him and let him hitch a ride as I kick and kick and kick.

"But the leggies!" yells Joe. "What if they catch us and eat us . . . or worse?"

"They're making a movie," I say, "not trying to catch us and eat us."

"But what if they're making a movie *about* catching and eating us?" whines Joe.

He might have a point there, but I don't want him to know that. So I change the subject. "What if Gregor the Gnasher is there? What if he's the star?"

I think back to the poster for *Parrot Fish of the Caribbean* and the picture of Gregor wrestling with the giant evil squid. I wonder what it must be like to actually be in a movie. I imagine that it's me up there on the poster and that I'm a world-famous movie star who lives in a huge house in Driftywood (where all the famous movie stars work and live). I start to grin as I picture being fed peeled shrimp twenty-four hours a day by my butlers, Rick Reef and Donny Dogfish!

But then it all goes wrong.

Suddenly, on the poster, the giant squid has grabbed me by the tail and he's using my hammerhead to bang nails into the side of a ship! My face starts to turn red, and I feel stupid for even dreaming that I could ever be cool enough to be a movie star.

Thankfully, I forget about my hammerhead once the huge, dark, open ocean approaches and we leave Shark Point behind. I can see the sunlight glinting on the tops of the waves.

WHAM! WHAM! WHAM!

The beautiful yellow light shimmers in time with the toots coming from Joe's rear as he gets more and more frightened. I look down at him, and he turns red, then blue, and then even yellower than normal.

Jellyfish do that when they're scared.

In the distance, Cora and Pearl are swimming as fast as they can. Normally, I'm one of the fastest swimmers around, but with Ralph and Joe slowing me down I'm finding it hard to keep up. Pearl and Cora are not only swimming around each other and high-finning when they come close, but they're also double-ending and tail-swapping as they go.

Up ahead I can see the shadow of a boat bobbing and skipping on the waves. As I look closer I can see a light brighter than the sun shining in the sea. There's a leggie dangling in the water, dressed in a rubbery wet suit. She's holding a massive light and swinging it around like the lighthouse on the shore above Shark Point.

SPLOSH!!!

Another leggie crashes into the water and I can see he's holding a movie camera. He's moving around, all excited, and pointing to the light-holding leggie. He wants her to shine the light over toward me!

My heart starts to pound. I let go of Ralph and Joe, smooth down my hammer with my fin, and give my best sharky grin.

The light shines right in my eyes and I strike a pose—just as heroic as Gregor in the poster, if a little hammer-ier.

But then it goes dark again as the light in my eyes moves away.

I look around, wondering what's going on. Here I am, all ready for them, but they're pointing their camera and light in completely the wrong direction!

And then I see what happened.

My heart sinks like an anchor.

There, in the spotlight, flexing his fin muscles and pointing his tail, is Rick Reef! He's triple-nosing from the slickest fin slide into the über-coolest gill slam I have ever seen. Even I have to admit it is pretty amazing, and I feel the bottom fall out of my world.

Just as the world falls out of Joe's rear.

"Sorry!" he says.

"Shh!" I hiss at him. Rick finishes on an old-school reverse dorsal, spins on his tail, and throws his fins wide.

Not only are the leggies following Rick's every move with the camera, but Cora and Pearl are screaming, "Rick! Rick! Rick!" in their best cheerleader voices.

"I guess we'd better go, then," says Ralph gloomily. "No one's gonna want to film us if we're up against Rick."

I hold up my fin. "Not so fast. I haven't

even started yet. There's no way I'm going to let Rick steal the spotlight. He's not the only shark in Shark Point!"

I kick away from Ralph and Joe until I am right under the shadow of the boat.

That's when Rick notices me.

He keeps smiling and waving to the camera with his fin, but under his breath, he says, "Swim on home, Anchor Face. They're not here to film a dork show. They want real sharks, like me."

I grit my teeth and flip into a double-endy.

"Harry," calls Joe, "be careful! That

boat has propellers. You don't want to end up getting demolished!"

Rick laughs. "See? Even your friends think you're a clumsy dork."

In the background, I can hear Donny Dogfish, Rick's sidekick, laughing behind his fin. I glare at him, trying to look tough, but it just makes my eyes cross and he laughs even more.

Cora and Pearl are still chanting, and suddenly I feel really annoyed. I'll show those dolphins, Rick, and most important, the leggies, exactly what a hammerhead can do.

I push past Rick right into the camera's

light. Curling up my tail and taking a deep breath, I begin.

This is what happens:

1. I do a perfect nose stall.
2. Rick chuckles and busts three gill slams.
3. Gritting my teeth harder, I swoosh a double inside-outy.
4. Rick shouts, "Easy!" Then he does exactly the same thing and finishes on an almost impossible outside-inny!
5. I race toward the boat's shadow and curl a wicked single flip.
6. Joe is shouting at me to calm down, but I'm not listening.

7. Rick is right behind me, doing a full-on eyes-closed belly rush!

8. Joe screams something about me getting too close to the boat.

9. I yell at Joe to be quiet and fall backward into a desperate upside-down devil smash.

10. I can see that the leggies love it. They are swinging their light this way and that, following Rick and me with the camera.

11. Rick starts whizzing in tighter and tighter circles. I can't believe what Rick is planning to do. . . . He wouldn't! He couldn't!

Rick does! I don't believe it!

He bursts out of the middle of a swirl of bubbles and heads straight toward the surface. I can see him looking back at me with big wild eyes, as he kicks with his tail as hard as he possibly can.

Cora and Pearl are cheering him on. Even Joe and Ralph are watching with their mouths hanging open as Rick whoooooooshes past the leggies and BREAKS THE SURFACE!!!!!!

Through the sparkling waves I can see his shivering shadow twisting in the air above the ocean. He does a graceful double nosey and tail touch, then SPLASHES back into the water. The leggies go crazy.

That's it!

Spin. Kick. Spin. Kick. SPIN. KICK. SPIN! KICK!! SPIN!!! KICK!!!!

BANG!!!!!!!

I'm heading for the surface too. I'm going double . . . no, three . . . no, four times faster than Rick did. I'm heading up toward the sunlight with Pearl and Cora's screams and Joe's "Noooooooooooooooooo-ooooooooooooooooooooooooo!!!" ringing in my ears.

SPLLLLLAAAAAAAAAAAAAAASH-HHHHHHHHHHHHHHHH!!! I break the surface and I'm out into the air!

Flying higher and higher.

I know exactly the trick I want to bust. A triple-goofy gill slap and tail flip.

I twist and kick, still rising. Twisting. Turning. Feeling the wind on my sides, smelling the unfamiliar salty air, feeling the rush over my hammer as I ripple and twist.

I've done it! A full stunt above the waves, in mid-air with room to spare.

There's no way the cameras are still going to be on Rick.

I'm gonna be a STAR!!!!!

Well, I would have been a star if it hadn't been for the following six things. . . .

1. I'd come out of the water too fast.

2. I'd pushed up too high.

3. I hadn't thought about my re-entry after the tail flip.

4. And . . .

5. And . . .

6. Oh.

I crash down out of the sky and land with a wet, breathless slap—right on the deck of the boat!

CHAPTER 3

I don't know who's screaming louder, me or the leggies. They're running in every direction, waving their hands in the air in panic. I'm on my front, trying to flip myself off the side, back into the water, and realizing that I can't breathe!

This is bad. Really bad.

If I had time and wasn't about to suffocate to death, I'd slap myself in the head with my tail for being so brainless.

All I can see are running legs, and all I can feel is the hot sun on my back and it is starting to dry me out! I have to admit to myself that Joe was right, which makes the whole situation even worse.

I try yelling to the leggies to help me, but all that comes out is a terrifying hiss that seems to scare them even more. A couple of them even look like they're about to throw themselves in the water to get away from me. I think they change their minds when they realize that there might be one shark on the boat, but there are hundreds in the ocean.

I manage to get one fin underneath me and lift my head a little, so I can see more of what's going on. I look around and see that most of the leggies are huddled at one end of the boat. There are two more leggies, a man and a woman, climbing out of the water. One of them puts down a camera and the other a huge light and they start waving their arms. They're the filmmakers from the water!

I don't think this is the best time

for me to show off, but I do try to give them a smile.

The woman screams and the man leaps back and nearly falls into the water. I close my mouth and frown. Why are they so scared? But once I have my mouth closed, they get a little braver and start coming

toward me with their hands outstretched.

Slowly, I try to move forward using my fins and tail, but I just fall back on my belly with a slap. The two leggies coming toward me take a small step back, as if they expect me to bite them. I wish I could explain to them that I'm really not interested in eating them. I JUST WANT TO GET BACK IN THE WATER!!!

I look at them with each eye on the end of my hammer and try my best to lie still. The leggies look at each other, nod, and start walking toward me again.

It's getting really difficult to breathe now, and I'm finding it hard to stay calm.

The leggies grab hold of my fins and drag me to the side of the boat.

The wood of the deck tickles my belly and I let out a giggle, which comes out sounding a little like an angry hiss. The leggies let go again, and I have to think of something really sad to stop the giggling. I picture Rick posing on a movie poster. It makes me feel angry rather than sad, but at least it keeps me from laughing.

The leggies grab me again and take me right to the edge of the boat. I swivel my eyes around and see that the really scared leggies are getting a little braver now. They edge closer to get a better look. The leggies heave me onto the side of the boat. I can see the ocean, all wet and inviting below me, and then the other leggies coming toward me.

A few of them are brave enough to give me a little stroke before I get pushed back into the water.

Thank Cod! I can breathe again!

But as the bubbles clear, all I can hear is laughter.

Rick is right in my face, clutching his sides with his fins. Big, fat laughs are coming out of his mouth in huge snorts. Behind him, Cora and Pearl are laughing too. They have their fins across each other's shoulders, and they are

laughing so much I think they're going to be sick.

"There he goes!" calls Rick as I swim away as fast as I can. "The shark so clumsy he can't miss a tiny boat in the middle of the ocean! You'd better get those hammerhead sensors looked at, Harry. They're obviously as cruddy as the rest of you!"

Red-faced and with hot tears in my eyes, I swim and swim and swim. I can hear Ralph and Joe calling me, but I don't care. I have to get out of here.

"How useless are hammerhead sharks?" Rick shouts after me. "A whole bunch of leggies to chew on, and he lets them push him back into the sea. Me, I'd love to eat a leggy air-breather if I got the chance. Not Harry, though. Harry is their *pet!*"

I don't stop for anyone until I get home.

I can hear Mom in the kitchen. Dad probably won't be back from his office yet—or he's still trapped on the sports center roof—so I might be able to sneak in without anyone noticing.

But as I try to skulk past the kitchen, my catfish swims over and starts purring loudly.

"Is that you, angelfish?" Mom calls from the kitchen.

I hate it when she calls me that.

"No," I say. "It's the Most Dorky Shark in the History of the Sea, and the leggy air-breathers have it all on film to prove it!"

Mom comes out of the kitchen, wiping her fins on a dish towel. "What are you talking about?"

So I tell her.

When I finish, Mom wraps her fins around me and cuddles me close.

I hate it when she does that, too.

Why can't she just leave me alone?

Can't she see I want to go to my room and sulk?

Mom wets the edge of her sea sponge with her tongue and wipes some sea-weed from my face.

"Sounds like you've had a rotten day. Why don't I make you a lovely dinner and then you can soak in the hot spring and I'll scrub your back, like I did when you were a baby? I have a really lovely new sea-urchin scrubber. You used to love that."

Could my day get any worse?

Well, yes, it could.

Mom makes me sit in the kitchen while she cooks dinner. "Since you're so upset,

I've made you a whole plate of leggie-shaped fish cakes and coral crunchies! They'll make you all better."

My dinner is so babyish that not even Ralph would be willing to clean it from between my teeth.

Not that I care about Ralph anymore. Or Joe.

I don't want to see anyone ever again. I'm way too ashamed.

When Mom isn't looking, I pour the leftovers out the window and make it look like I've cleared my plate. Mom goes straight back to the stove. "That's my hungry little starfish! I'll make you some more."

I hold up a fin. "No thanks, Mom," I say. "That was great, but I'm full and I'm tired. I think I just need to go to bed."

"What a sensible little starfish!" Mom beams. "How about I sing you a lullaby, then? That always cheers you up." I open my mouth but it's too late. *"Rock-a-bye Harry, on the sea top,"* she shrieks.

Aaaaaaaaaah! Of all the lullabies in existence, why did she have to pick the one that mentions the sea top?

"I've got to go, Mom," I say, swimming for the door. Mom blocks my way with her hammerhead and gives me a big, slobbery kiss. I close my eyes and wish that I was in a terrible nightmare. At least then I'd be able to wake up. But I'm not in a nightmare. Mom pats me on the hammerhead and finally lets me go. I swim to my bedroom so fast my dopey head gets jammed in the doorway. Once I finally make

67

it in, I slam the door and throw myself on the bed.

What a rotten, ROTTEN day!

I don't think I've ever been so embarrassed. Not even when Dad accidentally tripped on Queen Aquae the Third's robe and fell into her lap on LIVE TELEVISION!

That's it, I think, *I'm not going out again for this whole entire vacation.* If I don't go out again, I won't see my dad making a fool of himself as he tries to open stuff and make stupid speeches, and I won't bump into Rick and the dolphin twins. And I won't be filmed making a complete fool of myself.

There's tons I could be doing at home anyway. It won't be that bad to stay indoors for the vacation, will it? I mean, I'm a clever shark—I can find lots to do. I'll make a list to show you.

1. Um, I could . . .
2. No wait, I know . . .
3. It might be a good idea if . . . no . . . um.
4. This is turning out to be a much harder list to make than I imagined.

Whatever.

I don't care if I'm so thick headed that

I can't even make a list of what to do while I'm all thick headed!

5. I'm staying in my room for the whole vacation and that's that!

CHAPTER 4

Hmmmmmmmmmmmm!

I don't want to open my eyes.

Hmmmmmmmmm!! Hmmmmmm!!

I'm not going to open my eyes. I snuggle deeper into my bed and flip more sea-weed blankets over me with my tail.

Hmmmmmmmmmm!! Hmmmmm!! Hmmmm!!!

Then a bright light starts flickering in front of my eyelids, making the darkness all pink.

The light just reminds me of the film crew in the sea yesterday. I put the pillow over my head.

"Come *hmmmmmm* on, Harry. *Hmmmmm* it's time to *hmmmmmmmm* get up!" Humphrey, my humming-fish

alarm clock, is humming right in my ear. I'd been in such a bad mood last night I'd forgotten to ask him not to wake me up at the usual time.

"Leave me alone," I say from beneath the blankets.

"But it's time to rise and SHINE!" says Lenny, my lantern fish, shining his light right at my closed eyes again. He's swum under the blankets to point his light at me. Lenny and Humphrey are really useful when it comes to getting up in the morning, when you want to get up. But when you don't want to get up ever again, they're a real pain.

"Look!" I shout, pushing back the blankets and roaring up out of the bed. "I'm not getting up!"

Humphrey *hmmmmms* quietly and Lenny flickers softly. Humphrey raises his fin. "I . . . I don't want to argue with you, but you've, um . . . just gotten up."

He's right. I am out of bed.

Which is *exactly* what I didn't want to do.

Why does everything keep going wrong?

On top of that, I can hear someone coming down the hall outside my bedroom. It'll be Mom, with a special breakfast to cheer me up.

I. Want. To. Scream.

As the door opens, I dart back into bed and signal to Humphrey and Lenny to be quiet with a dark look that makes them both shiver.

It is Mom, but she doesn't have breakfast.

"Morning, angelfish."

Humphrey and Lenny start snickering behind their fins.

"I just wanted to tell you," Mom goes on, smoothing down the corners of my blanket, "that Ralph and Joe have been asking for you."

The last two people I want to see.

I groan.

Mom stops smoothing. "What's up, angel?"

I think quickly . . . then flop my fins out wide and stick out my tongue. Mom peers at it. I can see Humphrey and Lenny shaking their heads and hiding their faces in their fins. "I don't feel well," I say, flipping my tail slowly and painfully and coughing a little.

Humphrey can't help himself and *hmmmms* in disgust, but I flick him a "pipe down" look from the other end of my hammer as Mom places a fin on my forehead to take my temperature.

"I don't think I can even swim to the kitchen for breakfast," I say, coughing again.

"Well, you don't have a temperature," Mom says. "But if you don't feel well, you'd better stay home, and I'll put the sea-cow steaks I had out for breakfast back in the fridge."

Sea-cow steaks?

My tummy rumbles at the thought. But I can't get out of it now. I groan and turn over in bed as Mom leaves, saying "Maybe Dad might want them in a sandwich to take to County Hall."

Today is shaping up to be as rotten

as yesterday, and I haven't even left my room yet.

"Hey, Harry!" I hear Ralph from outside my bedroom window. "You getting up or what?"

Joe puts his tentacles through the gap in the window and unlocks the latch. The window opens wide and Ralph and Joe float in. Humphrey and Lenny float out, shaking their heads at me.

Joe hovers over the bed, counting something on his tentacles. "One, two, three, four, five, six," he counts out loud. "You do know that staying in bed all day is the seventh most dangerous thing to do in the world? What if there's a reefquake? You'll be tangled in your blankets and won't be able to get out. It's very, very dangerous staying in bed."

I push back the covers and sit up angrily. "I don't want to see anyone today. Not today, or for the rest of the vacation!"

Ralph and Joe look at each other.

"You're not still upset about yesterday, are you?" Ralph asks.

"Yes, Ralph, I am," I say, crossing my fins.

"Don't be silly," Ralph says with a smile. "Remember how we laughed at Joe when he got TWANGED off the seahorse in Shark Park? He didn't become all moody and say he didn't want to see anyone, did he?"

Well, no. He didn't.

"And," Ralph goes on, "what about when I went into the girls' bathroom by mistake on the first day of school? You and Joe laughed so hard I thought you were going to explode. But I didn't get all dopey and not talk to you, did I?"

No. He didn't.

I uncross my fins. A bit.

"Come on, Harry, it's only the second day of vacation. We have a whole week to have fun. Let's forget about yesterday."

Ralph has a point. I completely uncross my fins and get out of bed.

"All right," I say. "But we aren't going anywhere near any cameras, okay?"

Within a couple of seconds we're out the window and I'm calling to my mom in the kitchen as I swim past. "I'm going to the park with Ralph and Joe."

"But what about your cough?" Mom cries after me.

"It's much better, thanks."

"But what about your breakfast?"

"I don't want any."

"You haven't had any breakfast?"
Ralph looks at me, panic-stricken.

"Nope. Sorry," I say.

"If this keeps up, I'm going to waste away! I'll shrink from a pilot fish into a pilchard, and then where will you be?"

"I don't know."

"At the dentist with rotten teeth, that's where, because I didn't clean them for you."

"All right, all right," I say. "I'll have double helpings tomorrow, okay?"

Ralph thinks about this. "Okay, but I prefer seaweedies, not prawn flakes."

I sigh and nod. "Can we get going now, please?"

All this talk about food is making my tummy moan and rumble. I wish I hadn't pretended to be sick. I wish I'd gotten my teeth around Mom's sea-cow steaks!

When we get to the park, we're the first on the swings. We even manage to get Joe to take a turn.

Joe swings up high as Ralph pushes him and I swim in front, high-finning Joe's tentacles as he comes close. But

then Ralph gives one huge push and
Joe is sent spinning right over the top
of the swing and flying straight toward
me!

*PLAP. PLAP. PLAP. PLAP. PLAP. PLAP.
PLAP. PLAP. PLAP PLAP. PLAP. PLAP.
PLAP. PLAP. PLAP PLAP. PLAP. PLAP.
PLAP. PLAP. PLAP.*

. . . is the sound of Joe's tentacles

sticking to my hammerhead as Joe holds on for dear life and we fall back onto the seabed.

After that, the three of us are laughing so hard that I've completely forgotten about yesterday.

Except . . .

FLUBBERRRRRRRRRRRRRRRRRRRR!!!

Suddenly, my stupid hammerhead is boinging all over the place and I can't see a thing as my eyes swivel and shake.

"Hello, Rubberhead!"

It's Rick.

He's sneaked up behind me and flubbered my head with his fin. Ralph and Joe catch hold of each end of my hammer to stop the shaking.

Donny, Cora, and Pearl are there too, laughing at me as Rick circles around us. "Hey, it's Harry Hammer—the star of the funniest film of all time. Can't wait until that one HITS the theater!" laughs Rick. "It's going to be a MASSIVE SMASH, just like it was on that boat!"

Rick and Donny can hardly swim upright, they're laughing so much.

I'm about to tell Ralph and Joe that we should go and leave those two jokers behind, when suddenly something catches my nose. Sharks have the best sense of smell in the ocean, and hammerheads have some of the best senses of all the sharks, so I'm the first one to smell it.

It's a warm, fishy, tasty, yummy smell, and it's getting right in my nostrils. I can feel it sliding right down my throat and into my very empty tummy.

It is such a delicious smell. It doesn't just make my tummy rumble, it makes it almost shake with hunger, almost as if Rick has flubbered it!

I turn away from Rick, toward the direction of the smell.

Rick is a little annoyed by this. It's not the reaction he's expecting. He fins me on the shoulder. "Hey, don't turn away when I'm laughing at you!"

But I can't concentrate. The smell and the taste are beautiful, and my tummy is telling me to follow it, whatever Rick might be saying. I kick away and use my shark sense to lock on to the delicious aroma. I can dimly hear that Rick is following me, telling anyone who'll listen what a weirdo I am.

"Harry! Wait!" calls Ralph, but I can't help myself. When a shark gets hold of a scent, especially one as tasty as this, there's no stopping them. I must find out what it is, and I don't care what else is happening!

I kick faster.

"Listen, Rubberhead, if you . . . oh . . . oh . . . WHAT IS THAT SMELL?" Rick has obviously caught the scent too.

I kick even faster. Whatever it is, I want to get to it first.

"H-H-H-Harry!!" calls Joe. "Don't go that way! It's toward the open o-o-o-ocean!"

But I'm not listening to Joe, either. All I can hear is the rumbling in my tummy, and all I can smell is the tasty scent.

"Come on, Joe, we'd better follow them!" I hear Ralph calling to Joe, but I'm too far gone. I'm out of the park now, swimming faster and faster. I can hear Rick talking as he kicks faster too. "That is the most delicious thing I've ever smelled," he says dreamily.

I kick harder. Rick is not getting there first.

Faster.

Faster.

I can feel the drool coming out of the corners of my mouth. I want that food, I want it now, and I'm going to get it FIRST!

Faster!

FASTER!!

We're right off Shark Point now, out over the seaweed fields where the shepherd fish tend their flocks. The scent is dragging us down into the forest of seaweed growing there. But it doesn't slow me down. I keep kicking and I can feel Rick's breath on my tail.

He's closing.

FASTER!!!!

FASTER!!!!

In the dim distance, I can hear Ralph and Joe shouting, "Watch out!!! Harry, WATCH OUT!!!"

And then I can hear Donny shouting too. "RICK, STOP! STOP!!!"

But the scent. It's too strong. I can't stop.

So as I burst between the thick fronds of seaweed, it's much too late to see that I'm heading straight toward two wet-suited leggies, holding lights and cameras while floating inside a huge cage!

Rick and I are going too fast to stop! We're going to crash right into them!

CHAPTER 5

What happened next is a bit confusing, as you can see from the list that follows.

2. *WHAM! CRASH!*

   TWAAAAAAANNNNNGGGGG!!!

4. I go bouncing and boinging off into the deep.

3. My hammerhead doesn't get stuck. For once.

1. We both put the breaks on, but we hit the cage at FULL SPEED!

See what I mean? Completely confusing.

I've bounced off the cage and am somersaulting through the water. I flap my fins, desperately trying to slow myself down. Eventually I get control over my body, but my head is a whole other problem! It's vibrating worse than when Rick flubbers it with his fin. I shake my head and try to stop the movement, and after a few seconds the ocean stops rocking and I can start to make sense of what's happened.

The film crew has dropped a shark cage into the water and is filming from it. A shark cage isn't for catching sharks, it's to keep the leggies from getting eaten by the sharks they're filming.

"Mmmmmmmmmmmmmmmmmm!" For a moment, I think that Humphrey has followed me all the way from home, but then I realize it's me making that noise. I look down at my tummy and I remember how hungry I am. The smell of food that drew Rick and me here at full speed is

almost too strong
to bear. I turn on
my hammer-vision
and see that on the
seabed all around
the shark cage, the

leggies have poured buckets and buckets
of juicy, yummy, lovely shrimp!

They've obviously done it to get
sharks to appear, so Rick and I have
done exactly what they want. I don't
care, though. Opening my mouth wide,
I start to swim about like crazy, shovel-
ing in as much shrimp as I possibly
can.

It's the most amazing shrimp I've ever tasted, and I honestly can't get enough. The delicious scent of it is in my nostrils, and the taste going all the way down from my mouth to my rapidly filling tummy is just mind-blowing.

In fact, I'm so busy concentrating on getting as much shrimp as possible that I almost don't realize that someone is calling for help.

Swallowing hard, I turn my hammer-vision back to normal and see that Rick is caught in the bars of the cage!

The leggies seem delighted and are tickling him under the chin and patting

him on the head
as he struggles to
get free.

"Help! Help!" he
sobs. "Please get
me out of here!"

I can't help
laughing a little to
myself as I shark

down another mouthful of shrimp. Poor
Rick. I suppose I should help him, but
then I notice that the film crew is
pointing their lights and cameras right
at me.

I feel my cheeks turning red in

embarrassment as I remember what happened yesterday, and I start to cringe. I bet they're filming me because they're still making their movie about comedy sharks, and I'm clearly the most hilarious shark in the water.

I'm about to swim away and go hide, when I see the woman leggie reach down into the cage and take the lid off another fresh bucket of shrimp. She pours it into the water right in front of me, and then gives me a massive thumbs-up. She wants me to eat!

I dart forward into the cloud of tasty shrimp and barrel roll into a half fin curl.

The leggies applaud and lift their cameras and turn the lights on again. They want me to bust some more moves!

I don't need any more encouragement, and as I leap forward I have completely forgotten about yesterday and all the embarrassment. This is awesome! I'm finally getting the chance to show everyone what I can really do. I power up over the cage, twisting into a radical ninety-degree hammer shift (the move only hammerheads can do, and the one I never do around Rick because it always makes him flubber me). The leggies throw out even more shrimp as I turn that trick into a belly crunch and slide-swish right along the top of the cage.

"Harry! Harry! What about me?" calls Rick, still trying to get his head out from between the bars.

I rub past Rick and tail-tickle him, which drives the leggies crazy. They love it!

"Help! Help!" Rick cries.

"Har-ry! Har-ry!"

What?

I turn around, and I can't believe what I see. Not only have Ralph and Joe and Donny arrived, but Cora and

Pearl have followed them out of the park, and the dolphin twins are chanting *my* name!

Ralph and Joe are clapping along as Cora and Pearl chant.

"Har ry! Har ry!!"

And I'm off again, swishing up past the cage. Using my hammer as an extra fin, so that I can turn quicker and tighter than any other shark, I twist into an ever-tighter spiral.

Building up speed.

Faster

Faster.

Just like yesterday. But this time I'm going to be heading down.

Faster!

FASTER!!!!

And then *BANG!*

With the sun above me lighting the water in an explosion of glittering sparkles, I race down toward the cameras and the cage. I triple-gill, run three simultaneous back pikes, and roll into a totally cool three-quarter gnash master. With a whoop and a yell I fall past the cage, do a complete body stall, a gnarly nose-endy, a floaty inside-outy that goes straight into a perfect outside-inny that Rick would have been over the moon to pull, and then, to finish off, using the edge of my hammer as a lever, I POP Rick right out of the bars and out into the open water!

The leggies are going crazy. The light is on me, they're following my every

move with the camera, and they're kicking their last buckets of shrimp into the water all around me.

I spin up, openmouthed, through the shrimp, eating every bit.

As I turn back to the cage, I fold my fin across my now-full tummy and bow to the cage and the leggies inside. They've dropped their cameras and lights and are just applauding and cheering along with Ralph, Joe, Cora, and Pearl.

Rick doesn't hang around. I can see from his cheeks that he is just as embarrassed as I was yesterday. He pulls Donny away from the group and heads back toward Shark Point.

"Hey, Rick," Pearl calls out as he slinks away, "bet you wish you were a hammerhead, don't you? That way your pointy head wouldn't have gotten stuck in the cage."

Cora giggles. "I can see how much you scared those leggies, too. They were so scared, they could only tickle you under the chin!"

Soon Rick and Donny can no longer be seen.

And everyone else is laughing and cheering with me.

Except Ralph.

Ralph has pried open my mouth and is eyeing all the bits of shrimp stuck between my teeth.

"Breakfast at last!" he yells as he dives in!

CHAPTER 6

Ralph, Joe, and I are just about the last Shark Pointers to get into the movie theater tonight. It is absolutely packed.

We thread our way carefully between the rows, trying to get to our seats before the movie starts. I ache all over from those moves I pulled for the leggies in the shark cage earlier. It'll be a while before I do anything like that again, but it was a whole lot of fun.

I have a humongous tub of shrimpopcorn, and Ralph's got two, having decided to take a night off from eating stuff from between my teeth. I think this has more to do with the fact that Dad has finally given me my allowance and I am paying!

Joe is too scared of the shrimpopcorn machine to get close enough to pick up a tub, so he had some "nice, safe ice cream instead, not too cold, though, because I don't want to get a frostbitten tentacle."

As we get to our seats I see that Cora and Pearl are two rows in front of us. They've got their aqua-phones on and are seaberry messaging all their friends. Cora catches sight of me and fins Pearl, who looks up. They both smile and wave. Then they hold up their aqua-phones and I see that they're not just messaging their friends, they're posting pictures and videos of me pulling all those stunts on to Plaicebook!

I, of course, turn red. But luckily, in the dim light of the theater, no one knows except me.

Phew!

Girls.

I sit down between Joe and Ralph, just as the lights go down and the movie begins.

WHAM!!!

Gregor is there on the screen, all huge and white and toothy. And pretty soon he's wrestling squids, and sword-fighting narwhals and racing to save the damsel-fish in distress.

It's great watching Gregor up on the screen, and for a moment I think about my two days in front of the camera being a movie star. Yeah, it was great for a while, but when I think about my . . .

1. Aching fins (ouch)
2. Bruised hammer (ouchy)
3. All the flubbering Rick did with my hammerhead (ouchy boingy)
4. Pictures of me appearing EVERYWHERE (cringey)
5. How tired I feel right now (zzzzz)

. . . all because of one small movie I was accidentally in, I think that maybe I just don't have the energy to do it full-time zzzzzzzzzz . . .

Ralph and Joe wake me up at the end of *Parrot Fish of the Caribbean*.

As we swim back home I realize that even though I don't want to be a world-famous movie star anymore, and even though I missed my hero Gregor's first-ever movie, at least one fintastic thing has happened. This vacation hasn't been boring at all!

HARRY

Species:

hammerhead shark

You'll spot him . . .

using his special

hammer-vision

Favorite thing: his

Gregor the Gnasher

poster

Most likely to say:

"I wish I was a great white."

Most embarrassing moment: when Mom called him

her "little starfish" in front of all his friends

RALPH

Species: pilot fish

You'll spot him . . . eating the food from between Harry's teeth!

Favorite thing: shrimp Pop-Tarts

Most likely to say: "So, Harry, what's for breakfast today?"

Most embarrassing moment: eating too much cake on Joe's birthday. His face was COVERED in pink plankton icing.

JOE

Species: jellyfish

You'll spot him . . . hiding behind Ralph and Harry, or behind his own tentacles

Favorite thing: his cave, since it's nice and safe

Most likely to say: "If we do this, we're going to end up as fish food. . . ."

Most embarrassing moment: whenever his rear goes *TOOT*, which is when he's scared. Which is all the time.

RICK

Species: blacktip reef shark

You'll spot him . . . bullying smaller fish or showing off

Favorite thing: his black leather jacket

Most likely to say: "Last one there's a sea snail!"

Most embarrassing moment: none. Rick's far too cool to get embarrassed.

SHARK BiTES

Hammerhead sharks have a great sense of smell and are able to locate food easily.

The blacktip reef shark is bluish-gray in color and is usually found in the coral reefs and shallow lagoons of the tropical Indian and Pacific Oceans.

The pilot fish is carnivorous (eats meat, other animals) and not only follows whales, sharks, and turtles, but also ships so that it can feed on parasites and leftover scraps of food. The pilot fish came by its name because it was thought to lead, or "pilot," larger fishes to sources of food.

Jellyfish have been on the earth for millions and millions of years. They were here before dinosaurs.

Bottlenose dolphins are not fish; they are mammals. They breathe air, just like humans do.

The longest living creature on Earth is the red sea urchin. Some have lived more than two hundred years.

The largest coral reef on Earth is the Great Barrier Reef, located in the Coral Sea near Australia.

Sharks have been swimming in the world's oceans for more than 400 million years.

There are more than four hundred different species of shark, from the giant hammerhead to the goblin shark.

Sharks do not have bones. They are cartilaginous fish, which means their skeletons are made of cartilage, not bone. Cartilage is a type of connective tissue that is softer than bone. Humans have cartilage in their ears and nose.

The shortfin mako is the fastest shark in the ocean. It can swim in bursts as fast as forty-six miles per hour.

The whale shark is the largest shark in the sea. It can grow to be as long as sixty feet.

SECRET FILES
THE HARDY BOYS®

Follow the trail with Frank and Joe Hardy in this chapter book mystery series!

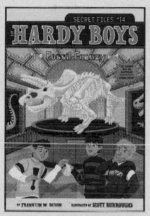

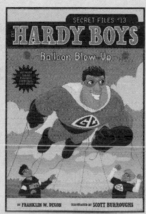

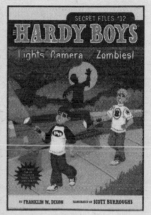

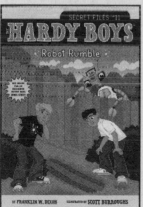

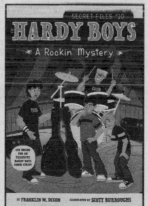

#1 Trouble at the Arcade

#2 The Missing Mitt

#3 Mystery Map

#4 Hopping Mad

#5 A Monster of a Mystery

#6 The Bicycle Thief

#7 The Disappearing Dog

#8 Sports Sabotage

#9 The Great Coaster Caper

#10 A Rockin' Mystery

#11 Robot Rumble

#12 Lights, Camera . . . Zombies!

#13 Balloon Blow-Up

#14 Fossil Frenzy

BY FRANKLIN W. DIXON

FROM ALADDIN • EBOOK EDITIONS ALSO AVAILABLE
KIDS.SIMONANDSCHUSTER.COM